Sleeping pill in a Storm

By
Alicia Humphries

W0017995

CONTENTS

Copyright

Author message

A Word from Your Author

This is a work of fiction all characters are fictitious. Any similarity to any person or persons either living or deceased is purely coincidental.

Alicia Humphries writes erotic fiction encompassing taboo subjects. She sincerely hopes you find her work entertaining.

If that is indeed the case then please visit the site you download or purchased this book from and leave a review.

For further titles by Alicia visit my Author Page at Amazon.

Many Thanks

Alicia xxx

Sleeping pill in a Storm

Leanne hates herself, well she doesn't hate herself, after all she's a bright beautiful intelligent young woman of twenty. What she did hate was her OCD's and phobias and today she surely hated her fear of thunderstorms. Like most of her fears It had griped her since she was a small child.

Today though was really going to test her. Usually when the weather was bad she slept in her mother's bed. Tonight though that particular comforter was not going to be available since an hour ago she and Garth had waved her Mum off on her business trip at Heathrow.

Her Mum had offered to call off the trip when the big storm had been forecast. But Leanne wouldn't let her, a decision she almost regretted now that she and Garth were driving back from the airport. Garth, her mum's boyfriend had volunteered to stay over to keep her company.

He broke the silence 'you OK gorgeous?'

'Yes I'm fine' she replied.

'I know you're worried about the storm, if it gets too bad you can always jump in with me', he chuckled.

Anyone else might have thought he was being cruel but she knew he was trying to lighten her mood. She turned to him 'I'll be fine. I'm going to have to face it one day' she said besides I've got Harvey. She was referring to her childhood teddy. She smiled, wanting him to think he was helping.

She also knew that it was a bit of a strange thing for him. He hadn't stayed in the house without her mother being there before.

They drove the rest of the way back to Lincolnshire in virtual silence. By the time they'd been out to eat at his favourite Italian and arrived back at home it was close to midnight.

She knew it was a ploy to get her tired, the wine and the lateness, she figured he thought she'd be so tired she would sleep through the storm. She knew that it wouldn't work she was already feeling her panic level rising. The first distant rumblings had started.

* * *

She got to the top of the stairs as he came out of the bathroom. All he wore was a towel around his waist. Any other time she would have been a bit embarrassed. She'd had a Bit of a crush on him since her mum had first brought him home the truth was she felt a bit jealous of her mother because he was truly a good looking man with a great body. Better than most guys half his age.

Tonight for the first time she didn't get the nice warm feeling in her guts about him she usually did..

He stopped on the landing and turned back to her. 'Leanne I have a confession to make'

'Oh?' She said questioning him.

He looked straight into her eyes 'It's about me and storms'.

His gaze unnerved her slightly.

'I too have a fear of them.'

'You're just trying to make me feel better. she said up to him

'No really I haven't even told your mum. I was kind of happy she asked me to stay with you. I can't stand being alone in a house when there's a thunder storm.'

She didn't know how to reply to this. She was supposed to be minding her! Well sort of anyway.

He opened his hand to show her three white pills. 'I take these, they're sleeping pills.'

'Three! On top of a whole bottle of wine?' She couldn't

hide her shock.

'Yes it's what I've done for years. It knocks me out. I'm guaranteed not to wake up for at least eight hours.'

She stood dumbstruck for a second.

'I've got more if you want some?'

Another of her phobias was pills, he probably didn't know that, she wouldn't even take a pain killers for headaches or period pains.   ' no not for me.'

She turned and went into the bathroom

'Nite,' he said.

She didn't reply she was angry and frightened. He was supposed to be here to support her and it looked like he was going to be out for the count. This was going to be one frightening night.

* * *

She lay under the sheets holding Harvey as tightly as she could. Another loud boom that felt like it was right over the house. 'One Mississippi, two Mississippi'. The sheet lighting lit up the entire room it was so bright that for a second she could see every detail of Harvey's hairy body.

She screamed, for the third time, Mum would've been in here after her first scream but she was still alone. She couldn't take any more. It was just wrong to be in this bedroom instead of mums during a lightning storm.

* * *

Once she was on the landing upstairs she hurried across to her Mum's bedroom looking over her shoulder as if being followed. At least he'd left the hall light on as he said he would.

She opened the door and went in leaving the door half open. Being in a dark room was simply not an option. He was lying on his side on her mums side of the bed his chest and arms exposed the covers down over his waist.

She got into the bed on her usual side, it felt comforting and familiar. It wasn't quite the Same, Mum would have given her a reassuring cuddle. Garth was right on the other side of the bed his back to hers. She closed her eyes and tried to at least rest. She knew she wouldn't actually sleep.

Another boom sounded in the night. Her eyes sprang open and she began to count again, four, and the flash was only half as bright she sighed in relief the storm was passing.

At the same time the thunder had struck Garth rolled over to the middle of the bed. One of his feet fell against hers. She felt a tingle at the warmth, she moved her foot, not away but to get more comfortable.

The storm got further away quicker than she'd expected. At some point, she couldn't put her finger on the exact moment, her anxiety had subsided. She turned to her side with her back to Garth and put Harvey on the floor beside the bed. As she shifted to settle for some much needed sleep so too did Garth, suddenly he was up against her back his arm across her and his face touching her neck.

He had spooned her in his sleep. Her thoughts turned to

him, turning over in her head her crush on him, it made the unlikely embrace a good thing.

She allowed herself to like the contact between them his knees against the back of her legs his chest against her back and his hot breath on her neck.

She noticed too that his nether regions hadn't quite made contact with her. 'Fuck' she thought, she was in her panties! How the hell had she gone to bed without her bra or nightie on? That was the thing about anxiety attacks you really were not yourself!

She'd have to go back to her room she thought. She lifted his arm and scooted forward, as she did he clambered onto her more, his hand fell on her stomach and he pulled her tighter. He kissed her neck, an electric shock ran from his lips right through her body.

Now she could feel his manhood pushing against her lower back. She hadn't even thought to wonder about what he was wearing. The shock was actually a pleasing one when she realised was completely naked!

His body heat warming her from top to bottom now, and especially at the top of her butt and bottom of her back.

His cock was the hottest part of him. She lay dead still not knowing what to make of the conflicting emotions flooding through her.

Any doubt about how to feel were soon gone. His hand spread on her stomach then he pulled her gently backwards and rocked his pelvis into her. She took a deep breath as a wonderful feeling flooded throughout her entire being. She'd never felt this way before with ex boyfriends.

He kissed her neck again and this time the electric current turned into a lightning bolt shooting through her, ironic she thought since the storm had brought her to this point.

She finally moved and nudged herself back almost imperceptibly against him. He let out an almost inaudible sigh of his own. Then she raised her eyebrows she could feel his cock starting to slide up her back as it stretched. Within a minute it was rock hard and pushed up against her.

She remembered her biology classes, men have on average six erections through the night every night of their lives. His hand moved up from across her navel, it came right up to her breast and cupped her, her nipples stiffened. She fully engaged and began to enjoy the whole experience. She moved gently applying pressure back against him.

His sounds of pleasure encouraging her, he moved too rubbing his cock against her back. She could feel small sticky deposits on her back. She smiled 'precum' she thought as her body responded in kind, and she dampened between her legs.

One of his fingers rested onto her nipple and circled gently around. Again he pushed his cock into her back and he kissed her neck. She squirmed, her reaction automatic. She panted quietly loving the nipple tease of his light finger. She wriggled against his cock more now feeling more and more sticky precum.

She was afraid to break the spell and yet she had become so turned on she needed more she needed to cum. She stretched her legs pushing herself up the bed until the tip of his cock was up against her knickers right by her asshole.

She reached down behind herself and put her thumb under the elastic waist of her panties. She pushed at the tiny garment. Her tugging obviously exciting his cock. He started to move more he too was panting. She was pleased of his movement since it allowed her to move her panties easier.

She pulled them down just enough to expose her ass. The front of them still in place. She paused. The effort had made her arm ache.

Then she got a second wind. She reached behind again. And for the first time her hand fell onto his cock. She wrapped her hand around it. Now he moaned, spurring her on. She was so horny now nothing would stop her getting what she wanted.

She pushed his erection and lifted her ass parting her legs at the same time. She forced it between her legs, once she'd positioned it he pushed forward. She pulled her hand out fearing it would be trapped between the two of them.

He pushed hard, his cock slid all the way along her slit and his cock head pushed up against her clit. She gasped at the intensity of the contact. She brought her leg back down trapping his cock the back of her panties trapping his balls.

He pushed back and forth. He slid along her pussy folds easily. The head of his cock parting her labia and bouncing against her clit, she gasped   and moaned more loudly than before.

The fiery ball in her gut spreading to her loins, his pushing was erratic lack of conscious control she assumed. It made the whole thing more intense. Not the usual rhythmic movements of lovemaking. Sometimes he even stopped completely before suddenly pushing forward into her clit.

The desire to cum built inside her. She moved with and against him her hand on him rubbing his thigh and ass. His hand still massaging her tit.

She tried several times to bend herself backwards and swallow his cock into her but she couldn't get the angle right.

His embrace just tight enough to prevent her from lifting up the bed enough, she settled after trying her manoeuvring one time to find that as he pushed forward. The end of his cock touched the very nub of her clit.

She daren't move. It was exquisite. The exact spot she touched when she masturbated. Only having his cock there was a thousand times better. She gasped each time he pushed and found it.

Then the storm picked up again. Just as he found the nub again, huge clap of thunder sounded right over the house. The room lit up so bright but she could not care less.

Having him, the object of her six month crush more to the point having his cock hitting the exact spot on her body that sent her wild took her over completely.

The rain had picked up again and was lashing against the window, when the second thunder and lightning struck it coincided with her orgasm. She pushed down on him as best she could as she gushed cum all over his cock.

He must have felt the hot juice. He certainly would have felt her legs crushing together around it.

He shot his lode too, his spunk filling the front of her knickers and smearing across her pussy and into the tiny piece of soft manicured hair.

His wrestling like hold gave and she lay in a delicious spoon embrace with him. Listening and watching the thunderstorm with a smile on her face.

* * *

Now back in her room other thoughts entered her mind. What she now associated with a storm was a pleasant event. She was cured of her phobia. Just like the therapist had said. Of course she could never tell her therapist the truth about this night. But she was dying to tell someone. That someone would be Cassie.

For now though the light of dawn was slowly building. The rain had stopped and the yellow glow appearing around the edge of the curtains confirmed what the weathermen had said. It was going to be a beautiful sunny day.

Getting any sleep was out of the question. She'd kept her knickers on soaked from herself and him. Now she pushed against the front of them smearing his spunk all over her pussy area.

She massaged her clit thought the flimsy cloth feeling his sticky slimy sperm all over her. She came two more times. Then she took off the panties rolled them in a ball and kept them in her fist and drifted off into a sleep. She dreamt of magical thunderstorms filled with Garth and sex.

* * *

The train shook from side to side violently, she looked outside the window and saw Garth hanging on to the side. He was calling something to her. 'Wake up, wake up Leanne'.

A second before her eyes opened she realised she was dreaming. She looked through the mist and saw Garth, his arm on her shoulder shaking her. 'What's up she said groggily.'

'Oh thank fuck I was worried, it's after midday and you didn't answer when I called you, I thought you might have taken some of my sleeping pills after all and... Well never mind.'

He looked to the ceiling and then just got up and walked out of her room.

She stretched, her mind following her body into wakefulness. Then she got what he was saying he was worried she might have OD'd. Then she understood why he'd looked up at the ceiling. She was laying on top of her sheets naked. Her scrunched up and now solid knickers on her pillow beside her face.

Her horrified shock quickly turned to glee. He'd pleasured her, although he was not aware of the fact, so why shouldn't he have seen her naked. She hoped he liked what he saw.

He put the eggs in front of her and some juice. ' I'm real sorry about last night' he said. Leaning against the counter

'Forget it' she said it's one of those things. 'Besides I think just having you in the house made a difference. I wasn't scared at all in fact.'

'So we don't need to tell your mum.' He said with a cheeky grin.

'No were good.' She reassured him.

'That's excellent. We won't mention Harvey either, we wouldn't want her to get the wrong idea.'

'Harvey?' she was confused as hell.

'He must've got into bed with me during the storm. He was on my bedroom floor this morning.'

She looked down at her plate.

'I assume you got in the bedroom and changed your mind right? Don't worry, I mean its not like anything happened.'

How much further from the truth could he be she thought.

* * *

Later that afternoon she sat drinking a cup of tea at caz's house her lifelong and best friend stared at her dumbfounded. They kept nothing from each other they saw themselves as souls sisters and they never judged. Leanne wondered if that was about to change.

'Fuck' Caz said.

'Want do you think.'

'FUCK!'

Don't just keep saying fuck. Leanne said with nervous impatience.

'I can't believe it, you lucky cow'!

'Lucky?'

'Yes you got to have sex with your hot, hot, hot soon to be dad.' I'm jealous.

'Wow, not the reaction I was expecting to be honest.' said Leanne.

'How long is your mum away for?'

'Two weeks.' She could almost see the cogs turning in Caz's mind. 'Don't get any ideas she smiled.'

'Don't know what you mean.' Caz smirked. 'You going to do it again?'

'No that was a one off.'

'OH OK.' was all Caz said in reply with a twinkle in her eye.

Now she and Caz were back at her place. Caz had unpacked her things. Leanne was speaking on the telephone. Caz brushed past her and continued chopping the onions that Leanne had left to answer the call.

Leanne hung up the phone. 'That was my mum'.

'She OK?'

Leanne ignored the question. 'He's coming over'

'What are you on about, speak English.' Caz said to her shaking her head.

'My mum told him to come over here and stay to keep me company. I told her that I didn't need company that you're here but she's already arranged it.'

'You mean the unwitting stud is staying here.'

'Yes.'

Leanne didn't know whether it was good or a bad thing.

Caz obviously thought it was great.

* * *

He'd been completely normal around her, she still had nervous doubts in the back of her mind, but the memory of last night kept making her smile to herself. She'd cooked and even cleared up after dinner. The three of them sat talking the entire evening.

They'd had four bottles of wine between them Caz had kept their glasses topped up going to the kitchen frequently.

Right in the middle of the conversation he started to nod off. 'You OK?' Leanne asked him.

He opened his eyes lazily. 'Yes gorgeous I'm fine just a bit tired.' He barely made sense.

'You want us to help you to bed?'

'Bed' he slurred. 'Yes bed' you know I had a naughty dream about you last night gorgeous.' He attempted a wink. He sounded drugged and drunk.

Leanne took a sharp breath and looked at Caz accusingly, Caz had her finger to her lip and had gone bright red.

'How many?' Leanne demanded.

'Four' Caz said sheepishly.

He'll be out all night. Leanne said. She tried to be angry but it was impossible. Caz was after all her soul sister. but four sleeping pills could be dangerous.

'And Viagra.' Caz whispered obviously a bit embarrassed.

'What!' Leanne was totally gob smacked.

'I got them from Granddad's bathroom cabinet before we came here.'

'How...' Leanne couldn't finish the sentence.

'I been crumbling them in his wines all evening, and don't tell me your not pleased.'

Leanne had to admit, although she hadn't thought of it herself,   now that the opportunity had presented itself the thought of getting more than just the taster she had last night was an exciting prospect.

'And did you hear what he said. He had a dream about you, well he thinks it's a dream and he obviously liked it.'

'How do we know he won't wake up.' All doubt gone from her mind Leanne now was getting into the swing.

Caz put her mouth to his ear and screamed his name. He didn't flinch. Then she slapped him across the face still no reaction.

Happy? Caz shot her a glance

Leanne smiled back. 'I will be when you get your tits out.' They'd experimented years ago together at college and now Leanne was becoming so horny she wanted to take full advantage of the situation.

Caz giggled and in a blur had her top and bra off.

She did have lovely tits thought Leanne full round and huge nipples.

Caz came to her and undid her blouse. 'Let's get you undressed too eh?'

Leanne let her friend take off her blouse and bra. They both stood facing each other. Leanne leaned in and kissed her friend. Caz responded opening her mouth and taking Leanne's tongue.

They came close. Their breasts pushed up against each other hardening their nipples.

Caz put her hand up and ran her fingers through Leanne's long auburn hair. Leanne responded in kind Caz' hair was shorter than hers and she stroked the fine mousy Bob.

Caz nodded towards Garth sprawled on the sofa. I see the blue pills are working too. Shall we relieve some pressure. Leanne turned to see what Caz was referring to. Garths cock was straining against his trousers.

Leanne got on the sofa on all fours beside him. She undid the button and zip and pulled back his shorts as best she could. Seeing in the flesh what she'd felt between her legs last night sent a pulsing right through her.

She leaned down to his face. She'd tried so desperately last night to kiss him and failed.

Now nothing was stopping her she the sensations running through her so similar to the panic attacks that she almost moved away.

'Kiss him Leanne' Caz put a reassuring hand on her shoulder. She moved the few last inches and put her lips to his.

They parted under her touch. She tentatively moved her tongue into his mouth. Hearing his moan made her shoulders and spine go cold. She moved her tongue feeling around his.

She noticed a slight temperature change on her ass as her skirt was lifted up and onto her back. Then Caz's fingers stroked along the sides of her butt, fingers went under the elastic of her panties and they we're pulled down her thighs to her knees. She lifted one knee then the other allowing her best friend to take them off.

She kissed him harder he kissed back equally. Amazing how you could perform these acts whilst totally asleep she thought. Caz's hands were now strokingbup and down the backs of her legs and her butt.

Caz had lovely delicate warm touch. She moved her own hand off the sofa and placed it in an arch over his half exposed cock.

She felt Caz's hot breath on her butt cheeks and her hands gripped and spread her. Then a sensation she'd never had before.

Caz licked her ass ring flicking feather like at first then applying more pressure. Finally the wet tongue pushed into her asshole.

She had to break from her kiss to get air. The tongue in her ass felt good. Not, make her orgasm good, but a damned close second. She pushed back letting Caz know she liked it. Caz forced her tongue in deeper in reciprocation.

She wrapped her hand around the top of his cock and Egan to massage stroking at the same steady pace she was being ass fucked by Caz's tongue.

Caz was not letting up. She felt a finger in her pussy now moving in and out matching the tongue and cock massage. Then Caz's other hand tickled its way up her leg and found her clit.

Caz stopped tonguing her. She felt a twist of the finger inside her and then another finger where the tongue had been. She pushed back and the second finger went in her ass

Caz pushed on now determined to finish Leanne off. The pounding fingers in her pussy and ass and the swirling on her clit brought her to a stomach heaving climax.

Caz's finger made loud slurping sounds as it was covered in her juice. She was just hanging on to garths cock now not able to move as the orgasm took hold. When she'd finished Caz withdrew and Leanne sat back down on her heals

Caz hugged her from behind and kissed her neck. She whispered 'was that OK.'

'Oh yes.'

Caz stood first. 'Let's get his cock out. I want some of it.'

They pulled and pushed and tugged until finally they had his jeans off.

Then his shirt they stood arms around each other

admiring him. 'He really is a gorgeous specimen.' Leanne said.

'Yes and for the next two weeks he's ours.' came the reply

It was Caz's turn to get on the sofa next to him, she scooted up right beside him and played with his hair. 'Kneel between his legs Leanne,' she rocked her head in encouragement. At the same time she lifted her legs up onto the sofa. Leanne saw that Caz's had taken her panties off.

She knelt between his legs as Caz had said. Caz kissed him surprised at his lively response.

Apart from his eyes being closed his body behaved as if he were awake. She finished kissing him and went down to his chest.

She licked his left nipple causing him to suck in between his teeth, she turned to Leanne and smiled then turned back and licked the other nipple soliciting the same reaction. She moved to the centre of his chest and then down to his stomach.

She pushed her tongue into his belly button, after she'd moved his iron bar of a cock out of the way. She turned to look at Leanne. She was stroking his balls.

'It seems a lot stiffer than it was last night.' Leanne whispered.

'Have you touched it yet?' Caz asked her

She shook her head.

'Go on then,' Caz looked at the cock only inches from her face. Leanne put both hands around it. She was amazed it felt so rigid 'how many Viagra did you slip him'

Caz did her sheepish look again. 'Three'

'Fuck me Caz.'

'Well he's got to satisfy both of us...let's stop stalling and come here. 'Suck the underneath of his bell end.'

Leanne went for it. As she attacked the base of his cock head Caz put her mouth on him too. They moved up and down his cock keeping both their mouths leeched on him.

Caz got to the top and took the end in her mouth. Her eyes lit up. Leanne pulled at his cock with both hands her top hand against Caz's mouth his whole cock was covered. Caz sucked like a starving woman.

Leanne felt him moving erratically under them she recognised the signs from last night. They'd only been servicing his erection for a minute.

'He's going to cum' Leanne said.

Caz looked at her quizzically, obviously disbelieving. Her doubt lasted about another two seconds his cum hit the back of her throat.

Leanne smiled and carried on milking. Caz sucked as hard as she could, spunk ran down the sides of his cock all over Leanne's hands.

After Caz stayed on the sofa snuggled against their

unconscious lover and Leanne layed between his legs. After a while they realised his cock was not getting any softer.

Leanne giggled.   'Those pills are magic.'

Let's not waste them eh.? Without waiting for an answer she pulled herself across him with her back to him she squatted down and lowered onto him. He gasped and shifted in the seat. Caz smiled at Leanne. 'Oh boy you are going to love this. It's harder than my fucking dildo.'

She moved up and down making his cock fill her. Leanne lifted Caz's skirt an moved in. She licked Caz's pussy and his balls.

Caz couldn't hold out for very long the deep fat grind on this perfect specimen of a man and the warm wet tongue of the best friend sending her nuts.

She froze as her body let go its tension. She held her breath and let Leanne lap up the juices that escaped down the side of his cock out of her.

Next it was Leanne's turn. They moved him around and lay him down.

Leanne rode him fast and furious. Her friend knelt being her arms around her waist and her hands on her clit.

The faster she fucked him the faster Caz masturbated her. Her climax threatened to rip her guts out. She screamed like a banshee.

They swapped and took turns, they milked his cock twice more. Caz came three more times on him and Leanne twice. Eventually his cock softened. The effects of the Viagra wore off.

When he was of no more use to them they dressed him, no mean feat he was twice their size, it took on them nearly half an hour to get him to a state that would not arouse suspicion.

For the next fortnight they drugged him every night. They abused his cock and each other. They'd drunk his spunk, fucked him eaten and fingered each other using both their imaginations to the full.

Cowgirl was great but they regretted that he hadn't actually been awake and actually fucked them. Sure they'd sat on his face plenty of times and he'd eaten them both like a professional.

But that was not the same as him getting on top and looking into their eyes or banging them as hard as he could doggy style.

'What we'd give for you to fuck us up the ass Garth,' Leanne said to him laughing on their last night then kissed him on the cheek.

'Back to normal tomorrow' Caz said to Leanne.

'Well I need a rest anyway. My pussy is sore from fucking him.'

'Mine too can't wait for your mum to go away on business and she's not even back yet.' They laughed.

* * *

Her mum had arrived back in the late afternoon, she hadn't stopped mentioning how much Leanne had blossomed in just a couple of weeks.

She wore makeup that really showed off her features and sexy clothes befitting a beautiful young girl.

The three of them went out to the Italian after Caz had gone home. Back at the house Leanne had stayed up for an hour after her mum and Garth had hit the hay.
She stepped from her bathroom into her bedroom. She froze.
Garth was standing at the end of her bed naked! Her mouth fell open. She looked him up and down even though she'd seen his cock for the last two weeks it looked bigger sticking out in front of him.

He said nothing. He lifted his hand and pointed the screen of his I phone at her. She realised in an instant that she was watching herself and Caz with him.

Finally he spoke. 'So you were so busy abusing me you didn't even look at the shelf in the living room, didn't you think I would notice my sleeping pills going missing? It was a rhetorical and sarcastic question.

Her mind settled as the implications dawned on her. Im so sorry Garth. What are you going to do?

Well I don't know what your mother and Caz's parents are going to say.

She went as white as a sheet. 'Oh fuck' was all she could say. He smiled a pantomime evil grin. Funny you should say that. I took your mother to bed and fucked her. Then I slipped her three sleeping pills. She won't wake up till morning.

She screwed her face up confused by what he was saying.

'As for me I've taken three Viagra. That's what you and Doctor Caz prescribed right?' She nodded slowly not really registering what he was saying.

Don't worry I've got a massive supply. I was given a bottle as a practical joke for my fiftieth birthday!

'Now I'm going to give you what, it seems, you want.

Go to your dresser and bend over. His voice left no doubt about how serious he was. She did as he demanded. She was excited and scared.

He came up behind her. Put his phone on the dresser. And spoke. 'From what I've seen these pills keep me hard for about two hours. Pity your friend isn't here to share the load this time!'

* * *

He looked down at her bent over the dresser her pink tartan mini skirt hem at the top of her thighs. Her tight white top had ridden up slightly to reveal a couple of inched of her lower back.

'I must admit. I was surprised you couldn't find a boy your own age to mess around with. I am thirty years older than you.'

"You're not going to hurt me are you?'

He smiled to himself. It wouldn't do any harm for her to be a bit worried.

'Be quiet. You've been a very naughty and will take the punishment you deserve. Now take your top off.'

She pulled her tee shirt over her head and dropped it to the floor, 'now your bra.' She followed his command again.

He reached down and pulled her skirt up and lay it on her back. 'Oh yes!' he thought. He'd seen this and more on the recording on his phone but he had been a passenger. To see her perfect little ass now was almost too much. His cock twitched at the sight.

He slapped her ass, hard. She yelped. He did it again and again she yelped. He slapped her with both hands as hard as he could a dozen times.

Her knees had buckled and she'd cried out each time. He bent down behind her.

Her legs were shaking. He put a finger under the gusset of her panties and hooked them away from her pulling them down her legs a few inches. To his surprise they

41

were soaked. So was her slit which had come into view.

'You like this?' He asked.

She nodded without speaking.

He pulled her panties right down and off. He moved his face nearer her. He drew in a breath through his nose. Ahhhhh another thing he'd missed, the sweet smell of her young pink pussy.

He moved to her, bent his knees, took his cock in his hand and wiped it up and down her slit.

She responded by pushing back slightly. As she did he hovered at her entrance. He plunged forward in one long thrust.

She screamed, he could feel by her response that she must've felt shocked pleasure along with a smattering of pain. He put his hands under her and grabbed her solid round tits. She squirmed beneath him.

He pinched both her nipples hard.

'Keep still it's my show tonight baby girl.' She stilled.

He stood still forced up inside her relishing the feel of her oh so young and very, very tight wet hole. His cock twitched inside her.

She moaned, he could feel every ripple of her pussy as it snuggled around him. He pulled back right back till the tiniest slither of flesh remained just in her.

He could feel the cold on the rest of his shaft as the air fell against him.

Then he rammed in again. This time without pause he began to pump the hell out of her. Squeezing her tits and pinching her nipples. She cried out for him to fuck her and he obliged.

She arched her back and he pulled her up to him she half stood now. She was pushing hard back into him as he thrust in and out of her.

Her legs bashing against the dresser knocking over makeup and aerosols, the dresser rocked on its legs items of all description fell to the floor.

Her screams got louder and louder. Then he felt the heat of her pussy increase. The slippery cave got even slipperier and she came on him.

It ran out of her and on to him. He felt her hot juice run down his thigh. Three more pumps and he came himself. It felt to him like a pressure washer banging into her. She screamed again. Oh yes cum inside me.

She bent forward and rammed back into him while he came.

* * *

She panted her head laying on her crossed arms on the dresser to

.

'Is it better when i participate?'

'Oh fuck yes.' she breathed

He pulled out of her and turned. He got he full effect now, she was an extremely beautiful girl. Her perfect tits heaved as she caught her breath. Her tiny waist and flat stomach led down to the small tuft of hair.

'Go and lay on the bed.' She smiled up at him and complied

He followed her and stood at her feet.

'Lie back. Lift your knees up and open your legs.' She smiled at him again.

'Now!' He shouted feigning impatience.

Her grin disappeared and she did as she was told. He could see the half fear return to her face.

'Play with your tits.'

She did just that. His cock hadn't softened. He knew it wouldn't he'd seen the evidence himself. He didn't realise until now how much it was going to ache from the strain though.

He knelt on the bed between her feet, bent over and kissed her. She responded lifting her head up and kissing him back.

While he kissed her he pulled her knees up as far as he

could, pushing them up beside her head, lifting her ass right off the bed.

He knelt under her, her butt rested on the tops of his thighs. He rocked back and forth

His cock bathed in her juices, slipping and sliding along her slit,
adjusting himself until he was in position.

She pulled her mouth from his. 'That's my ass.' she said her eyes wide open

He smiled and pushed forward. Not as violently as before but steady and unstopping allowing himself to be swallowed right up to the last inch.

She gasped and gasped as he entered and pushed on. Her hands fell and grabbed great fistfuls of sheets as she braced against the huge thing being forced up her asshole.

Once fully in he wasted no time. He began to fuck her. She relaxed beneath him. His arms went around the outside of her knees and under her back.

He lifted her off the bed and swung her onto him pounding her ass. He kissed her again flicking his tongue around in her mouth she panted like an exhausted greyhound.

'Get your hand down there and rub yourself.'

He felt her hand between them. He didn't slow his banging. Then she began to grind her finger into her clit, her knuckles moving against his abdomen. She came in no time at all. When she did he had to stop.

The muscles in her butt so strong they held his cock in a bear hug. She whimpered as she came beneath him.

When her orgasm had passed she relaxed, he pounded on.

Then he felt the thrill inside his body.

'I'm going to cum soon' he said to her. She smiled again. He pulled his cock out of her.

He pushed her legs flat on the bed and pulled her down under him. He sat up a dangled his balls over her mouth. She lent up and licked and sucked on them. He rubbed his cock hard and fast. Then he moved forwards and forced her mouth into his crack. 'Lick my ass' he told her.

Her tongue probed into him and lapped at him. Hot breath on his ass was so nice. He felt the orgasm building in his balls. He shifted back and pointed his cock at her face, he howled and shot all over her. It went in her eyes, up her nose some even went in her mouth as she moved around trying to catch it.

After it was over he sat back down and saw it was in her hair and on the headboard too.

'Now suck my cock! Suck it till you empty me one last time and if you do a god job. Maybe tomorrow I will eat your pussy.'

She took him and yet again did as she was ordered.

Fifteen minutes later she was swallowing his spunk.

He rolled onto the bed next to her. 'Now stand up and let me see you.'

She stood next to the bed. He reached out. He wanted to know just how soft the hair at the top of her slit really was. He stroked a finger across it. It was like the softest cotton wool. He admired her body for a few minutes.

'Tomorrow Caz will join us. And from now on I will service your mother from time to time and you me and Caz can do this whenever we want. How's that sound?'

She didn't answer with words. She knelt on the bed and kissed him. They kissed until the birds started to sing outside and the dawn light began to come. Then he went to bed.

She couldn't sleep. She couldn't wait to tell Caz her story, she knew Cas would be excited beyond belief.

She lay and masturbated herself to two wonderful orgasms before she heard her mother get up and start breakfast.

All she had to do now was be cool and look forward to tonight.

* * *

Afterword

Hi. I've loved writing this book and sharing it. Please leave feedback it's what drives us authors on to keep writing.

Visit Alicia's author page at Amazon to discover more about her and her books.

Thanks again for reading hope you enjoyed x

* * *

Other Titles

Mel & Chloe Get their man

Mel & Chloe. Making Claire come clean.

Mel & Chloe Go to school.

Mel & Chloe Daddy comes to school.

Mel & Chloe Home from school.

Mel & Chloe Get home schooled.

Mel & Chloe From behind.

Mel and Chloe Family affair.

Mel and Chloe One big happy family.

The Sleeping pill

The Wedding

The Sleepwalker

The thunderstorm and the sleeping pill

Dive in

Dive In

Two beautiful world class synchronised divers. A super rich ex gold medallist step dad for a coach and no mother around.

When the news reaches them that they have been selected to represent their country their excitement overcomes them.

What starts as a champagne celebration quickly turns into some tricky and intricate double teamwork.

Random Sample

This will be better than any movie you've ever seen Emily giggled. She stood about six feet in front of him turned and bent over. She spread her butt cheeks. He could see her asshole and hanging between her legs her lovely pussy. Her clit even larger now hung like an upside down half opened flower bud.

Immogen knelt behind her and to one side slightly so he could see. She slipped a finger into the wet hole then eased a second in and started to fuck Emily with her fingers.

Emily pulled her cheeks apart as far as she could. Immogen thumped in and out as hard as she could. He wasn't sure he could take much more. He had his hand in his shorts now rubbing his cock.

Again Emily screamed and shouted. Immogen turned and smiled at him 'get comfy Daddy take it out a play with it'.

He didn't need telling twice. He yanked his shorts down and his cock sprang out into the light.

The head a deep purple, full of blood, the shaft straining against the covering skin, his veins bulging. He started to stroke it straight away.

'Oh god' shouted Emily 'call him daddy again'.

Immogen winked at him. 'That's it stroke it for me Daddy!'
'Ohhhh again call him Daddy again'

'It's sooo big Daddy'.
This time Emily screamed as she came again. Her juice squirted out of her, it ran down and off Immogen's arm onto the floor.

Emily sank to the floor completely spent, she turned to look at him. Her eyes widened as she saw he really was stroking his cock. They had both known that he had a big one but seeing now fully hard in his hand was something else.

'Wow Curt it really is big. I like!'

He smiled at them both. 'I'm not going to be able to hold on much longer girls'. You carry on.

'The show isn't over yet.' Said Emily. She moved over to the sofa sat on the floor with her back to the seat cushion. She leaned her head back and laid it on the cushion near his leg. 'Immie come over here and sit on my face.'

This will be better than any movie you've ever seen

Emily giggled. She stood about six feet in front of him turned and bent over. She spread her butt cheeks. He could see her asshole and hanging between her legs her lovely pussy. Her clit even larger now hung like an upside down half opened flower bud.

Immogen knelt behind her and to one side slightly so he could see. She slipped a finger into the wet hole then eased a second in and started to fuck Emily with her fingers.

Emily pulled her cheeks apart as far as she could. Immogen thumped in and out as hard as she could. He wasn't sure he could take much more. He had his hand in his shorts now rubbing his cock.

Again Emily screamed and shouted. Immogen turned and smiled at him 'get comfy Daddy take it out a play with it'.

He didn't need telling twice. He yanked his shorts down and his cock sprang out into the light.

The head a deep purple, full of blood, and the shaft straining against the covering skin, his veins bulging. He started to stroke it straight away.

'Oh god' shouted Emily 'call him daddy again'.

Immogen winked at him. 'That's it stroke it for me Daddy!'
'Ohhhh again call him Daddy again'

'Its sooo big Daddy'.
This time Emily screamed as she came again. Her juice squirted out of her, it ran down and off Immogen's arm onto the floor.

Emily sank to the floor completely spent, she turned to look at him. Her eyes widened as she saw he really was stroking his cock. They had both known that he had a big one but seeing now fully hard in his hand was something else.

'Wow Curt it really is big. I like!'

He smiled at them both. 'I'm not going to be able to hold on much longer girls'. You carry on.

'The show isn't over yet.' Said Emily. She moved over to the sofa sat on the floor with her back to the seat cushion. She leaned her head back and laid it on the cushion near his leg. 'Immie come over here and sit on my face.'

* * * * *

Made in United States
Orlando, FL
22 March 2026

79568695R00036